SUHANI

SUHANI

TURIA

PARTRIDGE

To order additional copies of this book, contact
Partridge India
000 800 10062 62
orders.india@partridgepublishing.com

www.partridgepublishing.com/india

To,

You

For, you have found me

MIRA

I am about to deliver a lecture on the art of story-telling. As a journalist I have faced the camera so many times, however the idea of speaking before a live audience of a hundred is making me slightly nervous.

I try to remember the key points which I will need to elaborate on, nothing comes to me . . .

I close my eyes in desperation and breathe deeply . . . I see places, people and then a memory flashes by, I remember the Sadhu with dreadlocks on the banks of the Ganges in Benares, his parting note . . .

"Start at where they think it ends,

That will make your story."

Let's begin from the end . . .

I am a journalist by profession, but at heart I am a storyteller who loves travelling and exploring the unexplored. I have seen some uncanny things while I have travelled — an effeminate man going into a trance and revealing secrets about people around him, a tattoo artist who changed lives of people, a wizard who refused to accept his gift, a healer, a soothsayer, and now an artist whose art transgressed the wisdom of this world.

I believed that life was multidimensional, it was for the same reason that my stories centered around those who took their lives to another dimension. Suhani, however explored the inner worlds within those dimensions through her art. My first encounter with her remains fresh in my memory. In Tokyo, a friend dragged me to an abstract art exhibition; I had never been too keen about abstract art . . . the artist was Indian and I became slightly curious after having heard so much.

We walked into the gallery and I experienced something extraordinary. The paintings were not merely paintings, they were stories, many stories unfolding into one or perhaps one into many. The art took me by surprise. I, who did not understand a thing about abstract art was left mesmerised.

A painting that particularly caught my eye had a few lines written below, those lines will stay with me forever.

Beyond my window bars . . .

I see a star studded tree . . .

Alight with thousands of white lights,
breaking into the midnight blue fragrance . . .

Amidst those yellow threads
of faith on the tree bark

is an unanswered prayer . . .

I am waiting

I looked for the artist; I had imagined a middle-aged woman with a narrow face and deep set eyes, perhaps some grey strands, dressed in Indian attire. Upon asking around, I found in a corner a young woman in her late twenties with breathtakingly beautiful eyes. As I approached her, she smiled and greeted me. I introduced myself not just as Mira but as a journalist who travelled the world to discover and tell stories of the rare talents around the world. She seemed unusually amused at my introduction and I noticed the rise and fall of her perfectly arched eyebrows when she heard that I was a journalist. Clearly, she was very discreet about her life.

I thought it was best to leave the journalist in me aside and talk to her. She smiled as if guessing my line of thought and said, "I have nothing against journalists, just that I have always been discreet. I let the art speak for me, that's how it should be, right Mira? Slightly embarrassed I nodded and smiled . . .

We then spoke about mundane matters like the weather, nightlife in Tokyo, Korean food; all the while my mind relayed the beauty and light that her paintings brought.

One thing I needed to do was read everything I could on abstract art, and then, perhaps, I would know her a little better.

I knew fully well that artists were a slightly eccentric folk.

Six months have passed since then, I have met many people, interviewed a few, yet the memory of those paintings that had more to them than their physical existence has stayed with me.

Suhani had mentioned being discreet about her life, yet I wanted to know her better, perhaps to feel inspired, perhaps to learn something about art . . .

The Newsroom

The newsroom is in a frenzied mode, so infectious that everyone from desk to production seem like they are in an unending party. I am working on an interview with an author who painted his version of a controversial reality that has managed to irk half the nation. The author remains un-perturbed; courage is a virtue I respect!

While I finish my script and the questions, I get a call from a journalist friend in London. I smile as I see her name flash on my phone. After our usual enquiry into each other's lives, mundane matters and work gossip, she tells me that she has some good news to share. She happened to meet and interview an author who co-incidentally was in Tokyo, in that exhibition. He has agreed to talk to me. He happens to be the significant other of the artist I was looking for, maybe I could get to know her better through him.

I have something to start with, I know I will put together the dots, I always do!

Adding my share of happiness to the frenzy I dash out to meet my editor.

Place: London

A woman (journalist) in her early twenties makes way for a salt pepper haired and particularly handsome man. The man takes his place in the arm chair while the girl finds herself a place on the rug where she sits cross legged. He hands over a cup of chai to her, takes his own and smiles. Her eyes lighting up as she smiles, his not reaching his eyes. They are quiet for a while. She senses that he must be remembering something close to his heart.

He gives her a yet another fond smile and nods as if in approval. Mira asks him about his daily routine, his life as a writer in London and most importantly his story on the life of an artiste. She waits for him to break the ice . . . which he does; albeit with a smile.

They are sitting in a patio facing a lawn garden fenced by trees, there is an arm chair and a book with a strange book mark, cups of chai and spectacles.

He breaks the silence . . . "Let me tell you a little anecdote," he says. "A boy and a girl are having a late night conversation.

Boy: Have you heard Baul Music?

Girl: No, what is it?

Boy: Oh forget it, it deserves to be heard; in all its rhythmic glory, not explained.

Girl: Well; play it then!

Baul music plays in the background while the girl and the boy lie down, looking at the dark blue sky."

Girl: Have you ever wondered whether music feels; about how notes of music feel when they are played, or when they are not?

Boy: (Raising Eyebrows) Umm not until this moment.

Girl: Do numbers like it when they are divided, added subtracted, multiplied? Do colours like being on the canvas? How will we ever know?

Boy: Only if we could talk to them!"

Mira smiled as she heard this anecdote and wondered whether it was his personal experience or something he had written; before she could lose herself in that thread of conversation, he continued . . .

"Artists are a crazy folk, and I am saying this out of the experience of having to watch them very closely.

Oh! Are you wondering why am I saying this? Professional hazards I tell you. Had it been my way I would have been selling books at a store outside of London. And here I am in the business of storytelling; what a task it is indeed!

You see, this girl is an artist! Have you ever considered that colours could have feelings? Isn't life already complex enough? These artists are a crazy folk!"

Mira thought, Maybe, Suhani was crazy too and the reason I had travelled to London. Her story intrigued me, her life amazed me. So here I am writing from what I have known while connecting some dots between the known and the unknown. A storyteller must paint his story and a painter must carve it! So I will tell this tale as her and everyone who loved her and also those who didn't.

BENARES

The Sadhu looked into the eyes of the pilgrim who had travelled from far to meet him. Such powerful eyes, thought the pilgrim.

The Sadhu must have read that in his eyes.

The Sadhu smiled and thought, In your eyes I can see the lives you have lived, the journeys you have made, the people you have loved and those you have lost, the tales you told and those that you didn't; do not look into my eyes, for in your eyes I see the stories you have lived, when I see you, they become a part of me . . .

Everyone is a part of the same story, thought the Sadhu. After all life is a story, told and retold so many times, in so many worlds and so many lives . . .

SUHANI

The sun rose and birds called out from their nests. Still in a slumber, Suhani opened her eyes. What would today bring, she wondered. After a bath, she stepped out to clean the verandah. For the entire cooking and cleaning it took a good four hours. Once she finished the household chores, she sold tea and snacks at the Assi Ghat from morning till sunset.

As she sat at the banks arranging glass jars containing snacks prepared by her, her mind relayed a story about the journey of the jar that had gone through so much before finding itself in her hands. She made a mental note of painting it later in the day.

We all have our journey's to fulfil and lessons to learn, she thought.

The Sadhu came by and greeted her, she greeted him politely. He asked for tea and a bidi; she started to prepare tea and handed over his bidi with a slight frown. He smiled, a very rare smile. He was a regular at her shop, but he hardly spoke. Most of the time his eyes seemed like they were seeing other worlds. She returned his smile with a grin, she had so much to ask him but she was afraid of making a fool of herself. So, she decided to stay quiet as he continued gazing into emptiness. It was a busy day on the ghats, soon the pilgrims would surround the Sadhu and question him on life and existence. She would then listen in on the pretext of making chai for all of them.

On the quieter days, she would bring out her paints and canvas that she had purchased from the little money she had managed to save. The river, the sun, so many people from foreign land . . . nothing would exist in those moments. She would lose herself in those colours and their abstractness.

THE SADHU

The universe is leela - "a play," thought the Sadhu who wore a loin cloth and had his body smeared in ash. He watched the other end of the bank, boats were afloat closer to the other end of the bank, people made flower offerings, the ritual would soon begin. He saw the girl make her way through the crowd, it was the same girl who sold tea by the bank. A tall, dark haired, particularly handsome man made his way towards her . . . the traveller, thought the Sadhu. He looked up at the night sky, the stars had gathered for the ritual that had existed for thousands of years and will continue to exist till the end of time. We have all been here, thought the Sadhu and we will be here. It's the same story with different characters, puppets without a puppeteer, illusions without an illusionist, dance without a dancer and creativity without a creator.

. . . in the end we are all light!

MIRA

Rebuilding a story that happened almost five years ago isn't so easy.

The boat ride gave me a view of one of the oldest living cities in the world. It is fascinating to watch the seagulls soar in and out as the boat closed in at the bank. I paid for the ride and walked back to the hotel. Naga sadhus are a strange folk, I thought to myself. I had been a journalist for five years now and I had seen the good and bad of things. There were instances when I had risked my life to pursue a bit of information. Knowing stories and telling them to the world was my passion, it was for the sake of the same passion that I had travelled from London.

I go back to the hotel room; a stack of research papers on abstract paintings lay on the bed, in the corner of the room a wicker arm chair awaited me.

It is a strange world, at times nothing made sense, the abstractness of things is mind numbing and then on evenings like these, a sudden realization happens and everything falls into place. Yet, there is a beauty to the whole process, losing oneself just like striking odd notes, then one day the chords are tuned perfectly and a new symphony comes alive.

I have read almost every book on art that I could lay my hands on, knowing a story is easy, I think to myself, telling it to the world is not.

I fall asleep, as the evening wears on; tired yet peaceful!

In the morning, I walked from the hotel to the banks to catch a glimpse of the sunrise before heading to the house where she lived for 20 years. As I neared the Assi Ghat, I saw the Sadhu prepare his chillum. Instinctively, I walked towards where he sat. He did not look up, but smiled as the sound of bells from the nearby temples reverberated through the banks. "Do you know the significance of these bells?" he asked. I tried to remember if I had read some piece of information on it, I couldn't remember.

"They are to remind you that you need to arise, awake!" Lowering his voice he continued, "in the true sense, like a drop of water in a desert land, a reminder of the other side of the vast canvas!"

I take his leave after I promise to come back and meet him in the evening. Today, I will just walk around and soak in this city.

There is so much I have experienced in this city. I feel like I have lived a thousand years and more. Spirituality lives in these bylanes, I think as I walk through them. Each tantalising turn bringing a new pathway . . . A faraway sarangi . . . Like a bird calling out . . . or the twang of a sitar . . .

Calming energy that rises and falls . . .

The Sadhu laughs as I sit by the banks. Seeing him light his chillum, I ask him if he knew this artist and anything related to her.

He smiles, remembering her fondly . . .

"Yes, of course. More than her, I remember the deep dimpled man whose arrival changed her whole life or her arrival changed his, I can never decide.

She visited the banks since she was a child, with her mother at first; then for many years she came here alone, until one day she found him.

He was the anchor to her art, she the creativity to his consciousness."

Mira smiled and exhaled at last!

SUHANI

Assi Ghat

Almost sunset, it's time to close shop for the day. Silence has decided to make a pact with my soul ever since I have seen him. For the sake of that silence I must meet the stranger again. A flame has been ignited, now there will be luminescence . . .

It is evening; I sit at the banks looking at all the seagulls retreating, twilight is about to strike a chord with dusk, their play coming to a close, it is time for night crows and glow worms. I wonder how it would have been to be a seagull trying to soar up in the skies yet to be bound by the river lands. Is it difficult to break free from the roots? Won't the seagull learn about the skies and flying if he gives up his attachments? Maybe, in the world of seagulls things are simpler and needs are far more important.

I spot my neighbour and his wife taking seats for the ritual that happens every evening. Priests dressed in white worship the holy river in an evening ritual as onlookers participate in the chants and prayers. Women have covered their heads as a mark of respect; almost everyone has their hands folded. Lamps have been lit at the banks; the ritual will soon begin. It isn't my first time here; however, a certain someone has raised an emotion I was foreign to . . . "Hope" in its orange yellow fervour just like these oil lamps.

SADHU

There is this world and there are those other worlds, thought the Sadhu.

He saw the man smile a deep dimpled smile and the girl's eyes light up, after what seemed like a thousand years. He had seen her often, distressed, lost in thought; today was a different day, the clouds had parted, and the sun had shone at last!

Love is an energy and how beautiful are its forms, Prayer being the highest form. The Ganga Aarti was about to begin. More than a hundred revellers will go into a trance now, seep in faith.

Observing people while sitting at the Ganges was something he had done for years; it taught him a lot. He had seen people love, hate, rejoice, mourn. It's the same energy, he thought. The divine energy that cannot be created or destroyed, it can only be transformed. Strange are its forms, thought the Sadhu, as he took another swig from his chillum. Yellow orange lights flooding his senses, ancient wisdom seeping in, life's changing patterns, he thought; varied variations, concentric circles . . .

He saw the dimpled man sitting next to the thin, long haired girl, then his eyes moved to a mother praying for her child, and a friend feeling grateful for friendship. Every second this energy transforms itself into these moments, in this world and others; in this life and those others; in this love and others.

He thought about the first time he had seen a woman, the instant spark that hadn't gone amiss. He had to meditate for hours to be a witness to his rising emotion and the biological attraction. From then on, he always noticed the spark and its consequences in other people. In the years that went by, he had evolved beyond and could also see greater things now because he had surpassed greater experiences, but the spark had been his first tryst with understanding the ways of the divine.

Two strangers, however had just found the divine energy in each other for the first time. Often, he had seen eyes sparkle and hearts come alive which people termed as falling in love.

From here on, everything would seem like magic, nature's spell, the ultimate accident.

SUHANI

A strong earthy smell and a heart-melting grin greets me; I'm reminded of the Amir Khusro qawwali that played on the radio this morning — "With just a glance you have snatched all trace of me."

I look at the priests, the river, the temple and hundreds of worshippers; the river, perhaps is an excuse for a ritual that must have started even before the river ascended from the land of Gods.

He is staring intently into the gap between the raised lamps and the river. I try to avoid looking at him and make an effort of thinking about seagulls and the river, yet my mind drifts to him and so do my eyes . . . I wonder if my heartbeats are louder than these prayer bells by now. Why is this happening? And suddenly I feel long fingers close upon my wrist. "Brace your fears if you want to fly," he says. Does he know how to read the unsaid? I feel lost and protected at the same time!

KABIR

As she took in her confusions and looked upon the dying embers, he thought about the first time he saw her. Back in New York he would have discussed this encounter with his friend Joe. Joe was the saner one, the quiet student turned banker who seemed to know the everything of everything. He had drunk prophesied that Kabir would one day fall irrevocably in love in the most unexpected manner. Kabir was wondering if the prophecy was coming real. He wished Joe was around, to give him a hug and say "Hey man, this is it!"

Suhani's mind drifted from Kabir to her house, she didn't know whether she was going to be able to hide from them for long. It didn't matter anymore, she had nothing to lose and if she did; she was willing to give it up for Kabir!

They remembered the morning and the first time they met . . .

The morning boat ride made Kabir feel awake from the slumber that wore on for long after he woke up. As he got off the boat, he decided to have a cup of tea. As the boat closed in at the bank, he saw her. Her eyes, there was something about them. He felt instantly drawn to her and the moment their eyes met he knew that she felt the same. It felt strange, like forces of nature had brought them at that place and time, now they had to follow.

She certainly wasn't the first woman he had felt attracted to, yet he knew that this wasn't mere attraction; it was a connection that transgressed the body and beyond.

He had been with many women before; travelled continents, yet had kept his heart guarded. However, now with just a presence, all realities seemed altered.

Fresh smells of camphor and butter lamps filled the air. They didn't speak, not till the ritual ended. It was too divine a moment for anyone to speak anything and interrupt. Wish lamps made their way into the serenity of the river . . . so many wishes, thought Kabir; how many came true, he wondered.

His mind questioned everything and yet in his heart he had decided to allow things to happen and just follow the flow. He still couldn't fathom the idea of love at first sight, and the feeling of having known Suhani for many lives was also something he was struggling with. He had never particularly believed in reincarnations. Infact, he had never believed much of anything. He was someone who always questioned everything. For the first time, he felt like he knew the answers, perhaps he had known them all along.

The thing about hearts is that they have a language. In that language they unfold mysteries of this universe. We live to find ourselves after all, don't we! How can we find ourselves before risking ourselves first! That's the trick . . . It is a play, a leela where you play to lose and that loss is sweeter than all the victories, all the accolades. My heart beats for Suhani, from this moment on everything will change! I can sense it already!

I want her by my side, from this moment until the very end but I also want her to make a conscious choice, I know of her dreams and I want her to fight for them even if it means parting from me. I know I will be putting everything at stake but we can never possess those we love.

Growing up, I always thought that everything in the universe can be questioned. I have started to realise that sometimes the necessity of questions and answers disappears and then only void remains. It's in that void we must look for ourselves, perhaps that's love!

Two evenings later:

S he is sitting at the Assi Ghat feeding seagulls, humming a tune that Amma taught her. The tune makes her nostalgic, sends her back into the time when Amma sat by the hearth and hummed it; it seemed like a lifetime ago. Her eyes see the old world Benares in abstract patterns and suddenly she wishes she could share all of this with someone; her view of this world, her abstract art, her hidden life, and her tryst with inexplicable emotions.

For a moment, she finds herself lost in a whirlwind of emotions, calm strikes unexpectedly and suddenly everything falls into place. She realises that he must have arrived. It is like a game of shadows she thinks, their presence and absence altering realities. He smiles at her as he ascends those steps, it is heartening when she turns around to see him, her eyes telling him a story he has been longing to hear since they first met.

She feels happy to see him, they talk about the local guides and some locals Kabir has gotten acquainted with for his apartment. He finds her perspective about people intriguing. Usually, he makes a mental note about people and their traits, she on the other hand paints complex images that are difficult to fathom.

They talk about mundane matters; the local political party, the changes Benares has seen in the last decade.

It seems like the most normal thing except for the fact that they are like the chords set in a perfect tune.

They drink tea that he has carried in a flask which he carefully pours in a mug; seagulls are flying around, it is nearly twilight.

White clouds whisk above in surreal shapes, she doesn't know what to make of them. She sees him watching the clouds and wonders what he makes of them.

After some contemplation, he asks her if she would like a boat ride. She agrees with a nod, she hasn't had one for years now; her eyes turn melancholy at the thought. He helps her ascend into the boat and the ride begins. As they journey from one bank to the other into the sunset, he tells her about himself.

He was born to a gypsy mother who abandoned him when he was a baby, he was then taken in by a Catholic woman who taught him, sent him to school and made him family. His eyes smile, when he remembers his surrogate mother.

As he matured, his fascination for the art of storytelling grew and after he completed his studies in art and philosophy from the New York University, he decided to travel the world just like the gypsies.

The money that was needed for his travels came from doing odd jobs and freelance writing assignments.

"In an ordinary world," he says, "when the embers die and the lights are lit, when stars come alive and the moon beckons the night birds, ordinary people of the ordinary world fall into a slumber; that's when the wise ones reveal themselves to tell stories of the old folk around fires. I want to hear all the stories, the old and new, the wise and unwise."

She wants to hear them too, and perhaps bring them on her canvas. "It is time for the Ganga Aarti," she says. She must go back today but she will be back to hear his stories and tell hers.

He tells her that he has made a thousand journeys, but the one he is in is by far the most fascinating one; she listens to him slightly bewildered at his sense of saying the exact things that would make her uncomfortable. He perhaps senses slight discomfort and takes her hand in his, he then tells her that he wants to know her totally and he doesn't care even if she takes a thousand years to tell her story because he has made a thousand journeys, yet the one he is in has been the most fascinating because in this one he has met her.

SADHU

He had seen them ascend those steps; the deep dimpled man from a foreign land had helped the girl get into the boat. For people at the banks, it must have seemed like a thing to gossip about. Some may have thought of her as a prostitute, she hadn't realised it yet. She didn't understand the ways of this world, thought the Sadhu. He saw things that the world couldn't! For him, she had taken the most courageous step in her life. After all the spark makes people risk everything they have and even things that they don't. The spark makes them feel alive and that is the reason they fight for it.

The girl had been afraid, but she also knew that this was the most important risk she had to take. The man, however seemed a little perplexed. His aura revealed that he had gone through several experiences already, yet the spark had been amiss. This was the first time it had revealed itself in all its glory!

Did the man understand what was happening or was he letting-go so that the flow could take him through newer experiences? This was something the Sadhu hadn't understood.

The heart that risks the most lives the most, he thought.

Living and existing were different realities he had learnt about. He had seen many who existed for years, at times a hundred years. They were those who had never risked for the spark, who had never fought for their dreams, who had let the passive reality take over and let the moments of regret pass over them. These people existed in river lands and near seas, in deserts and in the mountains. They also tried to suppress those around them by instilling a fear of the spark. Why take a risk? The risk would always involve delving into the unknown and the unknown is always gruesome, scary . . . the known always comfortable. People existed in comfort for years and led those around them to do the same. There were a few who followed their heart; the heart always risks, it isn't afraid of failures. The heart rejoices, feels alive when it finds the spark in people, in dreams and in fulfilling things that the mind believes to be impossible.

These two had recognised that spark in one another, how far would they go in their quest to understand this mystery was a different story.

So many stories, thought the Sadhu, all illusions at last.

He asked Meenu for a cup of chai, and looked at the horizon as he prepared to peek into the inner world . . .

SUHANI

The thing with shadows is that they are cast upon by the sun like a spell in this mirage we live in. The sun's ways of connecting the earth and us, I think . . . I have always been intrigued by shadows, a strange beauty they bring, somewhat dark, yet they mirror, they follow and they remind that in the end, you are alone and it will always be about you in the end; nobody but you . . . yet you remain shapeless and formless and know that you will have to vanish someday.

What happens to the shadow of a person then when he/she falls in love? Does the shadow expand? I have never thought about this before . . .

Maybe, someday I will paint about shadows that fall in love. A love story of shadows, they are meant to do their karma each day and leave at day end as the sun sets, yet on a winter morning they decide to break the rules and fall in love. When shadows fall in love they cease to be what they used to be, they merge into one another and in that merging they expand . . . many universes becoming one and the one becoming many!

KABIR

He had been sitting and watching her lost in thoughts. She looked beautiful as she crisscrossed things in the farthest corners of her mind and arrived at where she wanted to. He wanted to watch her paint but he didn't know if it was the right time to express his wish. As if she had read his thoughts, she said, "I have been thinking, I don't get to paint that often. Will it be ok if I come down here and paint?"

"It will be absolutely fine," he said, taking her hand in his. He smiled at her, she smiled back a carefree smile. These were moments he would remember, he thought.

It was decided then, he would get her the necessary material and she would meet him in the school premises everyday once the school bell rang, where she would paint to her heart's content. She usually left for the house in the afternoon to buy a thing or two and run some errands. Meenu would take care of her shop while she was away, so there would be nothing unusual or suspicious about her leaving the shop that could raise a suspicion among her aunt or cousins.

SUHANI

I am sitting mindlessly at Assi Ghat; I must leave before everyone wakes up, but the sun is about to rise. "The morning marriage," Amma would say; the beautiful moment when sun rays fall on to the Ganges, sunlight gliding across the ripples before reaching the far end of the banks and waking the existence. At a distance, I see a man with jet black hair, smiling a deep dimpled smile, trying to feed seagulls while on a boat ride. I am caught up in that moment of the sun rising and his smile accentuating that moment as my heart skips a beat, something profound overpowering my senses. The boat is closing in towards where I'm sitting.

A smile, A nod, Greetings! Namaste, my name is Kabir and you are? Kind Eyes.

I am lost! Those eyes have taken me miles ahead; beyond body and being . . .

"Suhani," I manage; my heart has struck an unknown chord I never knew existed. I also thank Amma in my mind for her insistence on my English speaking skills.

Where are you from; why do you look so content; what are you so happy about; Life isn't so trivial you know! At least for some. I think.

He gives me a lopsided grin and asks me something about the Ganga Aarti (my heart skipping a beat with every word). It is a prayer ritual that happens at the banks of the Ganges every evening, I murmur something like that. By now he must think of me as someone stupid. I nod rather than saying goodbye.

A strange void-like calm has struck me, like the after effects of a percussion performance.

My heart is retreating into silence.

I reach home.

Colours where are you? I need you . . .

I quickly take out my canvas and colours. Red for this profoundness that has taken control of me, deep brown for the kindness in his eyes, a spark of blue for the connection we shared in that instant. The more brush strokes I make, the calmer my soul grows.

He asked me if I could explain the ritual to him in person, and without a thought I agreed. Something about him was very arresting, I was no longer myself.

I do not know how to control the strange emotions my heart has evoked.

The evening is as most evenings are; Pain, more pain . . .

Strangely I associate pain with the same colour I associate love with . . . Maybe love too gives pain . . .

I will never know!

KISHOR

S he was hiding it, but he knew that there was something that was making her happy. It had been two days, the pained expression on her face had been replaced by something else. He couldn't fathom the change. He had to find out.

Ever since they had moved to Benares he had found her presence annoying. Her patience and ability to tolerate was unbearable for him.

The more he plotted on mistreating her, the calmer she grew.

How did she manage this, but this time it was something else.

Something that gave her strength and perhaps . . . Security . . .

That was it! She had found a man for herself, something his father was not going to be happy about.

Life was different earlier, all we did was pass snorty comments on the pilgrims and while away our time. When we moved to uncle's house in Benares, father insisted on getting Suhani under control, it seemed like a personal task for him. I never really understood how or why Suhani dealt with everything silently and never created a ruckus. If I were her, I would have killed for freedom. All I did was follow father's instructions for his threats were never empty and nobody wanted to face his wrath, neither Ravi nor I!

SUHANI

As she returns from the Ganga Aarti, the alleyways are deserted, it is getting colder every night. She makes hurried steps, worried that she might land up in a problem. In her heart she is ecstatic, but her mind is worried. She opens the big iron door and then the small wooden one. Inside, there are stone steps leading downstairs to the hallway. In the middle of the hallway, there are four stone slabs placed around a circle of rice grains. She crosses the hallway mindlessly in an attempt to get to the kitchen only to find someone blocking her path. When she looks up, her heart freezes and sends chills down her spine; she looks down at the ground immediately.

It is her uncle, he is reeking of alcohol. She feels the bile rising in her throat, her palms have become moist and her breathing sparred. His eyes search for the scared expression on her face. Like an animal who has understood that his prey has panicked and is helpless, he grabs her and drags her to the adjoining room. She has given up screaming, it increases her pain. She becomes a corpse and lets the tears fall.

She heads to her room after resenting to the pain in her body and mind. She takes out her canvas and brushes and makes some distinctive yet repetitive strokes with red as the background.

It had happened every night since Amma had died and her uncle and aunt had moved from Allahabad. She had cried in vain, tried running away a few times, begged in front of Sahab, it had all gone in vain. In return she had been severely tortured, ridiculed and Sahab had conveniently ignored the whole episode.

She knew that things would change, Amma had taught her about faith in the darkest hour. She had merely followed Amma's lessons . . .

Her attempts at trying to get sleep were futile, thoughts were endless, they refused to go away. There was also a fear of losing herself, but that would mean losing nothing, she thought. Amma had taught her that there was nothing to lose, we came from nowhere and we had nowhere to go to. She kept rewinding her memory to the moment when she had first seen Kabir, she had never felt like that before, it was too overpowering. She felt like she didn't have the control over her mind and heart, she felt like everything from now on would belong to this stranger who she had just met. It took her sometime to come out from that trance.

His eyes were so kind, when he smiled she felt like something in her was healing, slowly but effectively, strange numbness taking over. She was happy and sad at the same time and didn't know what to make of these incidents. She let the tears fall, and wished that Amma was around to explain to her the meaning of this all or just reassure her that it was normal to feel this way.

KABIR

At the chai shop, cardamom tea spiced with black pepper and lemon boiled from a kettle from where the shopkeeper sat, the vapour rising, its shadow on the wall seemed like souls rising up from a cauldron of death. Strangely, it made him think about his life and the turns it had taken. If someone had told him he would travel to one of the oldest living cities in the world someday, and fall madly in love with an exotic woman from the ancient land of India, he would have laughed. The experiences that life makes us go through are strange indeed, he thought to himself.

He didn't know a thing about her. There was so much he wanted to ask her, so much he wanted to say. He sipped lemon infused tea from a tiny translucent glass cup, the liquid clearing his mind and comforting his heart. It was like the hesitation one has when playing the first note of music; once the chord is struck the artist realises the magic that will be revealed, fears disappear only love remains.

Suhani's Aunt

The days begin and end in the same fashion they have for a thousand years. Times change, places and people evolve but the river remains its surreal self. The garden needs to be mowed, dried leaves burnt along with the garbage, a heap of clothes need washing. I know that it is unfair that it is Suhani who will need to finish all this alone, but if my husband or sons notice my leniency, I will have to face the wrath, which I am not willing to. If that happens, I will not be able to protect her in the subtle ways that I do. They speak of terrible things, like selling her off to a landlord. I have kept them at bay by cribbing about the household chores. I know what she goes through and my heart goes out to her. I thank the heavens that I don't have a daughter, my husband would have been as terrible as he is with Suhani. When will this end! Is there any escape for her, I wish there is, this is not the life she deserves.

SUHANI

She is making a patchwork quilt for him, nights have become colder. Sunlight is flooding into the room as she picks and repairs pieces of cloth from worn out clothes, picking a combination of bright and soothing colours. It feels like she is recreating her life, pulling out the best of what is left and rebuilding it with more beauty and grace. The thing about patchwork quilts is that every little piece in it carries a story, every little piece in it has journeyed its way into being a part of the quilt. So many stories embedded in one, or one story embedded in so many . . .

She hums the music that she has heard him sing, she is not thinking about the future or fretting about the past. The quilt is a gift of the present, her way of being grateful for his love. It carries memories, it also carries parts of her that she has found and put together.

The high ceiling echoes her tune, she thinks about what he had said on their first visit to the Ganga Aarti "Brace your fears if you want to fly."

She had not understood what he meant then, love brings so much courage, she thinks . . .

KABIR

He was sitting at the Assi Ghat, his third consecutive day of his waiting for her. He sees her at last; dressed in red, head covered, she wasn't looking up, quite strangely. She walked past him without looking at him even once or turning to look at him; he was puzzled and slightly taken aback. She walked till the end and then gave a slight nod. Was he supposed to take that as a cue and follow her or was she hinting at him staying away. It was confusing. He decided to go with his instinct and followed her, keeping a safe distance between them as he walked on. She reached a narrow pathway and made a quick turn, it was an unnoticed green patch. She looked around once to check if someone had been following her. Seeing that it was safe, she sat there. Taking the cue, he went and sat beside her. She wore a maroon scarf and her face seemed deathly pale, her eyes had the same spark that he had seen when they had first met.

As soon she took off her scarf, he understood the reason of her wearing it in the first place. There was a deep red gash below her neck and several nail marks on her throat. A bile rose in his throat, who would have done such a horrid thing, he felt anger and deep helplessness for letting her leave that day. He looked at her intently not knowing whether asking her about this would be appropriate. She had seen his face change its colours, going from anger to pain to guilt. He looked at her and placed his hand on her head, tears made their way from her eyelashes to her lap. He let them fall on his shoulder as he took her in his arms, his caresses reassuring her.

As the sun set on the Assi Ghat, a girl with the red scarf had just experienced her tryst with sunlight and she had waited for long for it to dawn upon her.

The stars are countless and so are these moments that we have spent away from each other, thought Kabir. Each moment like a skipped heartbeat bringing back a thousand memories, shades of love, Suhani thought!

For Kabir it was as far as he could have taken her in his quest for the love he had in his heart. He looked at the scattered leaves that were being whisked away by the wind. Don't we all go back to where we have come from? The leaves came from the tree that came from the soil, the leaves will go there! What was the purpose of their life? He thought!

"To bring hope, by giving shade to a traveller in the sun," said the Sadhu. "What about love, then?" asked Kabir. "It is all energy, the same energy that helped the plant bear fruits, helped it bear branches that gave shade to the tired traveller in the hot sun! It's the energy that has changed its form, from love to hope and hope to love again!" said the Sadhu. He then laughed a fond laugh and bowed to the setting sun with folded hands, his eyes brimming with gratitude for the universe.

At a distance, the sun turned many shades of orange before becoming an incomprehensive abstractness, giving its last ray for the day and settling into the faraway waters . . .

After many days of walking around in search of a house that would fit in the scheme of expenses, Kabir found the one he had in mind. It was a simple house on rent with a view overlooking the Ganges. It was spacious with walls that were plastered in blue and the ceiling was high and dome-like, giving the place a very earthy feel. The parapets were a surprising yellow, he would have to ask Suhani to paint something on them. He liked it here, it somehow felt safe. He was just about to water his newly acquired plants when he heard a knock. He smiled his deep dimpled smile and went out to open the door. There she was, she smiled a tired smile. He heaved a sigh of relief on seeing her smile, it felt like soft sunshine after a night of storm. He knew he could breathe now. He didn't know how to broach the topic, he wanted to tell her that she didn't have to worry about anything ever, yet he knew it didn't seem right at this time. He wanted to know about everything but he knew she was hurt and it was best to let her confide when she felt right. She was with him now and he would do his best to make her feel safe.

Nobody said anything for a while. She sat down staring at her knuckles, not knowing where to start. She didn't want to seem like a needy girl who was throwing herself at him. She liked him, but knew her limits. They hadn't spoken that day even after the sun had set, that made it even more awkward.

She looked at him, she knew she was risking a lot by revealing her past and present but she had never felt this way about anyone and so she decided to follow that feeling. Exhaling sharply at once, she said, "I know you have a lot going on in your mind, I am going to narrate to you every chapter that my life has seen. I know that it is going to take great courage as I relive some moments and let go of some as I narrate them."

He saw pain etched across her face; he told her that it would be alright if she didn't want to talk about it.

A night before when he sat in his balcony, he saw hundreds of prayer lamps afloat in the Ganges. All of these have existed for thousands of years and they will continue to exist long after I am gone; then what could possibly the purpose of our lives, he wondered. Leaving that thought, his mind picked another stray thought that wandered all evening. Suhani! There was something more to her than this, he knew it. The connection they had made in one instant felt like the most important thing to him. Chance encounters were one thing, these were dealings of the heart. Would he ever understand the mysterious?

He thought about the places that he had been to and the strange things he had experienced. Women he had met along the way, some he had loved; however, he knew he had journeys to embark upon, newer experiences awaited him. Every time a bridge needed to be burnt so that a new one could be built for him to traverse upon and see a new world that awaited him at the other end. It seemed strange in the beginning, these short encounters, making friends with strangers and then not knowing when he would see them next. Yet, he knew that he carried a million memories in his heart. A million stories that would remain with him, cherished and treasured all his life.

Suhani, however was not merely a story for him. She was more than that, this was a bridge he wanted to keep for a lifetime . . .

This was the canvas she always assumed would remain untouched.

She got up and made her way into the kitchen, he followed her there. She found the zig-zag patterns on the wall intriguing, a lone kettle at the far end of the kitchen looked like it was in deep contemplation, sunlight from the open window poured in to make its handle glisten, giving it a slightly pensive touch.

"Pour water into the container. Let the water boil. Add some sugar, some spice and tea leaves. Let it simmer. Strain it. Pour it into cups. Serve.

This is the recipe of life," she said, as she continued to strain the last drops of tea from the residue. She smiled as she handed over his cup, looking intently at him. As she did so, their gaze met for a moment before she looked away; it was unnerving even after so many days.

"Some Sugar, Some Spice and Bitter leaves to heal your soul. Always treasure it," Amma used to say. She smiled, fond memories flooding like sunlight on the kettle. "Amma was my foster mother who took me in when I was abandoned," she started. "I really loved sitting by her side. Though whatever she said didn't make any sense then, it was very comforting to be around her. I would love watching her for hours with rapt attention as she went about her daily chores."

"At that time nothing made sense, but all those lessons have taken me a long way."

She smiled at him, he returned her smile not taking his eyes off her as he did so.

They sat on the orange rug he had laid in the balcony from where they could spot seagulls soaring in and out.

She looked at a seagull that seemed hesitant to dive into the water and began from where she had left . . .

Those were different times, I must say; not quite difficult but different, uncomprehending times . . . for a moment she found herself adrift in that time.

This is where it all began . . . under that Raatrani . . .

The Raatrani is where my fate and destiny were decided . . .

Sadly both coincide at some point . . .

I was born and abandoned on the same day by a mother who was too ashamed to face the world after bearing me.

Taken in on the same day by a man and his wife, a religious childless couple . . .

It feels like everything has happened right here before me and yet seems like a distant passing memory . . .

It isn't about memories, it is just growing past and beyond things that have shaped you.

Her opening up to him had been a very courageous attempt for her; somehow showing her a mirror she hadn't seen before, a part of her that she wasn't accustomed to seeing. She had never made any friends when she had gone to school, sharing secrets was as new for her as was falling in love with a man.

She addressed her foster father as Sahab; he was a wealthy landlord who had loved his wife once. As time passed, they realised that they couldn't have a child of their own. They went to temples across the country and fasted as many times as they could, yet nature refused to bless them. She remained grief stricken and he turned desolate, in that isolation grew a bitterness and ugliness that never left him.

He changed his ways and became a philandering man who had turned so bitter that he often hurt her physically and in other ways. Taking Suhani in was his way of keeping his wife distracted while he was away. After her mother passed away, Suhani's life changed for the worse. Her father asked his brother's family of four to move in with them for reasons Suhani never understood. It was fine in the beginning, her brothers despised her and so did her aunt. However, it didn't matter as she would spend her time in her room either painting or reading some of the old books.

One day she heard a knock on the door, it was her uncle. He had been nice to her, she smiled at him wondering what it was that he had to say. He entered without asking and closed the door behind him. She looked at him and in his eyes she read the dread that would take place. He forced himself on her on that day and on many others, forcing her to take a medicine afterward that would eliminate any chance of pregnancy. She knew he feared the neighbours. He beat her up if she cried too loud, and on the occasion when she complained to her foster father, he was so drunk that he passed out before she could finish what she had started to say. She realised that there was no escape and she would be free only when the time was right. She suffered in silence, doing all the household chores, not saying a word. Her tea shop was the small escape she got as a result of her silence. She narrated all of this with a straight face, she didn't want him to feel she was weak.

Without looking at her, he took her hand and cupped it with both his hands; she rested her head on his shoulder, they sat like that the entire evening. Nobody said a word, his eyes brimmed with tears, he let them fall . . .

AMMA

Suhani was the best gift life had offered Amma. Raising her was the most joyful experience for her. That's why she fought everything in her way to impart to her daughter lessons that she had learnt. She didn't know what would happen to her daughter once she left this world, but she had faith. She knew that her daughter would put to use everything she had learnt someday.

Alas, she couldn't fight death.

She thought to herself . . .

"My daughter is the best gift life offered me, and I have cherished every moment of it; watching her grow gives me immense joy that I will forever cherish. Sadly, I am unwell. I do not know if I will be around to protect her and raise her the way I have dreamt of. It was perhaps my karma to bring her in, and teach her everything that I have understood.

Sahab is away on his personal escapades; it's so much of a relief. I have imparted everything that I have known; now it's Suhani, who will have to take these stories forward and make them her lessons for life. There was nothing more I could teach her. My ill health worries me, what will become of my daughter once I leave this world. Will my lessons be enough? I can only leave this world with the faith that goodness prevails, always!"

KABIR

It was the darkest hour of a dark, dark night, so very dark that even the night crows shuddered to come out, the river had fallen silent, maybe she was listening to the leaves whispering. The banks were deserted, except for the Manikarnika ghat where pyres burnt all night. A man sat there and watched body after body being cremated. A strange emotion had taken over him, it wasn't sorrow, perhaps a strange vacuum that he couldn't comprehend. He felt like a man in a desert who had wandered aimlessly for years; only to find desert ahead. What would he do now? Where would he go? Everything began and ended with nothingness after all! He had realised that far too often, but this time he wasn't able to live it.

A naked man, the Sadhu with ashes smeared all over his body looked at him from a distance.

He understood at once that this man knew things beyond the realms of the ordinary world. He took in a deep swig from the chillum, marijuana reaching his lungs, filling his insides. He felt mindless, free, like the seagulls. The spot between his eyes throbbed and he smiled to himself; the third eye knocking, he thought jokingly.

The man at the banks got up to leave, wiping his watery eyes. It had been an intense experience, and he would perhaps someday write about it.

The Sadhu beckoned him the moment he saw him leave. His eyes were glazed, he seemed perplexed after he was called. However, for the Sadhu, that expression wasn't new, it had imprinted many faces after being beckoned. As he saw him walk, he saw his aura energies change, sunset yellow changing to ochre coming towards the heart and creating a defence. The Sadhu laughed, as the man came and sat on a mat facing him. He started the conversation at once, "Hi Sir, did you want to talk to me? I am Kabir." The Sadhu offered him a chillum which he politely refused; he was starting to get slightly worried now.

"Brace your fears Kabir if you want to fly," the Sadhu said looking at him. Kabir's heart skipped a beat. He looked at the Sadhu for a second to make sure he wasn't hallucinating. How could he have known, was it a coincidence? He looked at the Sadhu for answers. The Sadhu saw the dilemma Kabir was going through, he waited patiently and then began, "The truth will always remain the truth, it isn't mine or yours, yet it is for me and you."

"The truth isn't always easy, and if it were, it wouldn't continue to remain the truth. To overlook it and act passively is easy, to see it in its whole totality and then wear it on you isn't," he said pointing at the ash on his body. Kabir knew what he was trying to say and yet there was a plunge he had taken within and just like the highs are too high at times, this time the low was too deep and he didn't know whether he would be able to manage resurfacing.

"Have faith, Kabir," said the Sadhu. "Only faith will see you through in times like these, for after the darkest hour comes dawn," he said pointing at the horizon where the first beam of the sun travelled through the waters reaching a crescendo and then spreading light.

The Promise

"**P**romise me that you will not give up when the going gets tough," said Kabir. "Promise me that you will not be afraid to take a risk so that you can do what you were born to do, even if that means having to die for it, because what else is worth living for."

The sun was about to set, it was dusk; Suhani looked at the Ganges, nodded and said, "Yes, I promise."

She seemed a world apart from what he had seen her the first time, maybe it was the light, or perhaps she was now finding herself.

Now, it was his responsibility to help her, even if that meant losing himself or her. It was a risk he was willing to take.

In fact, that risk felt like the most important thing to him this moment.

He had to plan this thoroughly, an escape route to freedom. As she left that evening, he lay on the rug and let his mind do its magic all through that night and many nights after, as he discarded ideas after ideas to pull her through this.

SUHANI

She wakes up at dawn, and goes out to check if her cousins have woken up. After seeing they are fast asleep, she goes out to clean the verandah, the stairs, the circular room with the stone slabs, methodically dusting and wiping every possible nook and cranny. She then gets to cleaning rice grains and putting them aside. Dough kneaded and vegetables chopped, she starts with the frying, roasting, steaming, and cooking. By the time she finishes, it's time for the morning prayers.

It is as mundane as any other day could have been. She looks at the house one last time; she leaves with Amma's old saree, a few clothes and the passport that Kabir has managed to procure for her. Her aunt is sitting in the verandah looking quite morose. Suhani realises that for the past few days or weeks, her Aunt hasn't said a word to her. In the past she had observed that her aunt said mean and nasty things only around her cousins or uncle. Had she misinterpreted her aunt?

Her aunt looks at her searchingly, her eyes trying to unravel the secrets that Suhani had kept hidden somewhere deep inside. A point arrives where the search ends, somehow hearts connect, eyes reveal and secrets are spilled. It all depends on the intention of the seer. Her aunt for the first time heaves a sigh of relief and tells her, "Go in peace and never come back again. May God be with you."

Suhani tries searching for a hint of malice, a stray mean element, she finds nothing. She nods and leaves the house knowing she will never return.

Ever since Amma had passed away, all the household responsibilities had fallen on her shoulders, which meant waking up at dawn to clean the house. Upon failing those, she would have to be ready for another merciless beating by thugs who were supposedly first cousins. After Amma had left the world, Sahab had gotten his younger brother and his family of a wife and two sons, both whimsical to a level she couldn't imagine. Her aunt made sure that she did all the household chores or faced their wrath. Living there was like facing hell, and she never believed that life would ever be any different. She had known life to be like this and accepted it.

For Ravi and Kishor, Suhani was an outsider who they needed to punish for taking up space in the house and being an unnecessary burden. They had also been conditioned by their father who knew that slight sympathy could lead to Suhani getting out of his control.

Sahab knew it all, yet he neither had the patience nor the inclination to care for Suhani.

Smoke rings and soaring kites

He is lying down next to me on an orange rug that I have grown extremely fond of. His earthy scent mixed with marijuana is heady. The smoke rings he is puffing out, look like tiny clouds across the clear blue sky that we are facing from this roofless hideout. I wonder, at how drastically life has turned around and given me the courage to do something that was unthinkable earlier. What is this strange emotion, this endless longing, this beautiful energy that tests my limits and makes me want to cross them. While I am wondering about this, I see a purple kite soaring, going wherever the wind wishes. If the kite did have any emotions, would it feel the same way about wind as I do about Kabir; would that be the reason to follow the wind's path to wherever he would take it or would it be because the kite has seen the wind, now there is no salvation.

He holds my hand as a very casual gesture while he tells me stories from around the world. He must have done this so many times, I think. For me, my heart skips a beat with his smallest touch.

As I listen to his travel tales, the kite that I had seen adrift earlier is now soaring further away into the white clouds. Tiny kisses on my forehead are distracting my line of thought, blurring my vision. I cannot see the kite anymore. Seagulls soaring past from everywhere, it's about time. I must get up to leave. Strong hands, firm around my waist, pull me to them. Two breaths becoming one, soft lips and a tender, gentle kiss that speaks a million emotions. A lone tear escapes the corner of my eye.

Far above, the kite is lazily soaring across.

It is not easy to explain your emotions to someone when you view this world in abstractness. I need to learn more about the abstractness that engulfs my inner and outer world, about bringing the existential present and beyond on my canvas.

I must bring everything on my canvas, the said and the unsaid. I must prove Amma's faith right that in the end goodness prevails.

I know it takes courage to strive for that plunge into the sea of goodness. I must let go of all my fears and trust the man I love. It is a risk, but if I don't risk anything now, nothing will be worth living for!

Part 2

I am running down a deserted alleyway, my legs hurt and my chest feels like it's about to explode from this pressure. Fear in all its ferocity is trying to win the war with the courage in me. It's an inner tussle and I won't give up. I promised Kabir that I will do everything it takes and I will keep my word. Suddenly, someone grabs my dupatta. I do not want to look back to see who it is, my heart is racing. I let it tear away and run as fast as I can carry myself. I have reached a dead-end, now there is no escape; the sky above turns from clear blue to muddy dark. I scream, that's my only escape, even if I die screaming I won't regret and I collapse.

Frail hands on my forehead; I feel care, worry through them.

I wake up to see sunlight shafting through yellow curtains, sun has peaked it's way from the snowy mountains, the pond is reflecting its happiness at seeing the sun and the trees are swaying away in the energy of it all.

I have woken up! Or is it a dream.

I cannot seem to be able to let go of my past and embrace this moment, right here and now. I am drowned in sadness, sadness of the past, of the life that I have lived till now. My arriving here still seems like a dream to me, maybe I will wake up from this beautiful illusion and come face to face with Ravi or Kishor to be beaten and scarred.

The events of the past few months come back to me, my escape from Benares seems like a miraculous reality that I simply cannot fathom. I had walked into the police station shortly after I left home, narrating every incident and submitting all the necessary medical reports. The police arrested my uncle and cousins and charged them with sexual and mental harassment. The court case had been fast-tracked after some local media raked up the issue. Justice by punishment was Kabir's idea, I knew that Karma would also act, but I felt the need to restore my dignity and hence this was necessary.

They were imprisoned for 14 years and I was free, freedom is such a strange feeling. I was free but I wasn't liberated, not yet!

Kabir sent my work to art schools around the world, filling up applications, using all the necessary connections.

Maybe the Ganges was pleased with me or the Gods were too happy, we received a letter from an art school in China. Not only did they offer stay and facilities, the travel, too was gratis!

I had never seen Kabir so happy. He was like a proud parent that day, happy yet sad. Happy because I now had a chance to realise my dream and sad because he made me promise much against my wishes that while at the art school I will not try to contact him. If we are fated to meet again, we will; but if not, I will continue to walk the roads life puts me on. I have some wonderful places to see and great glories to achieve. I never understood why he did that, but I will wait for him.

GRANDMA HUAN

A woman in her eighties dressed in a wraparound bottom and turquoise silk shirt examines me, she doesn't seem too happy. Maybe she witnessed all the nightmarish screaming. I try to explain in signs that it is ok. She seems sad, as if her old mind is trying to find answers.

It has been three days since I arrived here, it still isn't sinking in somehow.

I get out of bed, I have about an hour to get dressed and eat. My formal training in art starts in an hour, informally I have been training ever since I opened my eyes and saw this world. My life is about to change forever, morning's hope taking over the deep sadness that the night presented me with. I miss Kabir!

I had just about two pair of clothes when I got here. Grandma Huan with whom I will be staying as a guest as a part of the residential art school arrangement has given me some of her freshly laundered old clothes. To me they are a blessing, like everything else is. I wear a similar wraparound bottom with a white top and tie my hair in a tight bun.

When I head down for breakfast, it feels like a tourist spot; people from different ethnicities sitting around in circles enjoying the morning sun.

I pull out a ladle and pour myself some soup. Slicing out three pieces of bread, I carefully apply butter; then locating a corner I go over and place my meal. I eat like I have never eaten before; food calms my gnawing nerves and warms the coldness that yesterday's nightmare brought in. It is a pleasant day, I see people laughing heartily, walking up and down with their sack of paints and brushes. Who would have thought I would be witness to this scene someday? The turns life takes are phenomenal!

The Teacher

We are sitting in the most unusual classroom I have been in, in a clearing of bamboo grove.

A lone canvas stands in the center of the clearing; everyone makes way and sits facing the canvas leaving some space in between.

At a distance, I spot a middle aged man walking swiftly in our direction; a boy of twelve following him with two rucksacks. Something about the way this man walks is intriguing; he walks beautifully as if he were walking on water. I watch him sitting there in the bamboo grove, his shadow gliding gracefully behind.

A precise bow, and he gets to work. He neither addresses us nor introduces himself.

The class has fallen silent, the only sound is of the wind whispering through the bamboo trees. This is my first lesson here, in a completely foreign land. Isn't my teacher going to tell us anything? It has been years since I left school, maybe learning has changed now. One look around and I notice that others are equally bewildered, but nobody says a word.

The teacher has painted the entire canvas black, and in one swift moment he paints a moon white incomplete circle. To me, it seems like a cluster of stars in the night sky. Few students gasp, the rest are gaping, giving uncomprehending, puzzled expressions.

Another swift bow and the teacher leaves.

I am home. Grandma Huan has prepared a delicious broth, which is very welcome in this cold weather. "Evenings are breezy and cold with occasional drizzles," she says.

She must miss Grandpa a lot, I think. She lights oil lamps as the evening progresses and retreats to her room. I am left with nothing to do, it seems like a new life. I can afford to just sit peacefully in this house, doing nothing. Maybe, this is how it feels like to be home.

I decide to make the best use of this time and read the books on philosophies around the world.

The world and its happenings will maybe make some sense to me one day; with that thought I drift into a dreamless sleep, the first of many.

THE TEACHER

"An empty circle can encompass the universe in it, yet remain empty, 'spaceless'. Being able to paint the universe and yet remaining spaceless is an art that we can master and once we do, the universe will flow through us into our art; pausing he swished as if commanding some magic and smiled . . . and back. So let us all first empty ourselves," he added.

I noticed he was rather tall for an Asian man and his eyes crinkled at the edges as he smiled, as if they were reassuring us, emptying us slowly.

He then went on to explain the symbol of Zen, an offshoot of Buddhism which marked an incomplete circle in a single stroke.

Why was the circle incomplete? What did it mean? I wondered.

"Our lives, he continued with a slightly higher pitch are full of emotions, and as we make this journey we live them. These emotions also die by the time we come to the end, what remains is? He posed a question to the class, there was complete silence, nobody volunteered to answer this.

As if reading most of the quizzical looks across the room, he smiled and announced, "is for you to tell me in our next class."

He dismissed us after giving us our first assignment of each of our insights on the symbol.

I was happy to take back something to work on, I thought to myself. That would keep my thoughts away from Kabir. As we stepped away from the grove, a slightly older girl walked towards me and smiled. I smiled back, it had been awkward right from the beginning. I had not gone by myself to speak to any of the others in my class, I felt a little stupid about it now.

I made a few friends at art school, we would often spend our evenings sitting at the bamboo grove, watching the sun set.

The school inculcated discipline in us but it also set us free in many ways. It is here that I learnt the art of liberating myself and the others through painting.

"It is never about you alone," our teachers would insist; "but in the end it will always be only about you." So never forget, "it isn't just about you." These were some of the things that I would keep a note of; even today I am still trying to understand them. Maybe, with time I will fathom that which I have learnt.

Inner Calling
and revisiting the past

The canvas had remained untouched for weeks. I was reading up on philosophies, the cultures that were born out of them and lives that were moulded to fit into those philosophies. It was all very fascinating for me. The winter break had started which meant sparing fifteen days for the family. Since that was no longer an option, I gladly took on a task of helping the librarian in sorting the books and taking out time to read some of them.

As I leafed through them, a new universe opened up to me; a universe that was unlike the one that I had delved into when I explored the canvas.

There was Hinduism, there were traditions including the Shamanic traditions, the ways of the Aborigines, the Mystic ways, the Sufi sects; the more I read, the more amazed I was, yet there seemed to be something that held everything together. Colours of the same palette I thought!

Kabir would have been happy to see me turn into a voracious reader. Grandma Huan was away at her sister's place for a month. That gave me ample time to lock myself up and read, there were times when I fell asleep without realising I hadn't eaten a thing the whole day.

I knew that there would be a time when I would feel reborn, the art in me would reignite. For now, it was time to contemplate and do what was necessary.

Catharsis

A very attractive woman, possibly in her fifties sat near the fireplace. Suhani closed the door behind as she entered the sitting room. She had been summoned by one of the evaluators after she had submitted her final work.

The woman had beautiful eyes, but one couldn't look at her for too long for it felt like those eyes could see all that you had been hiding from the world. She signalled Suhani to take a seat in the chair opposite hers. Suhani did as she was asked to, her heart was racing. What if her work wasn't good enough?

"Never doubt the art within you, my dear," said the woman. She had a soft voice, a contrast to her bright eyes.

Suhani was slightly embarrassed. Had she made it so obvious for the teacher to notice?

"Your paintings are brilliant, you were born to do this is what I can say without   the slightest doubt," she said as she got up and walked to pour a glass of water for herself. She took a sip and smiled at Suhani. The girl has seen a lot in one lifetime, she thought.

"I wanted to tell you something," she continued. Suhani was starting to get anxious. "Your paintings, my dear are not a medium for your catharsis. Yes, they are a medium of expression and as artists we do have the liberty to express our inner world. Don't you think there is something beyond the situations that life has shown you and the emotions that you have witnessed as a consequence . . .

Art exists so that we can go beyond illusions and see the truth. If you get caught up in the illusions of this world and the situations of one lifetime, how will you manage to look beyond?

Will you repeat the same story with different characters each time you paint? The world is immersed in illusions, they will be fooled of course, perhaps even mesmerised. What about you? For how long will you fool yourself?"

"The greatest creative artists in the world experience something called the creative block. It is a strange paradox because creativity can never be blocked, it is abundant energy. The artist is in a block because he has retold the same story over and over again. The world has loved him, they are awestruck, now he has to cast another spell but how will he do it, he doesn't know a thing about magic.

There is this world and there are those other worlds, you have the power to harness them all and express them on your canvas. If you recreate what has already been created through you in your life and the situations you have gone through once, the magic will be lost.

It isn't one static point, my dear. It is a process . . . you will learn.

But first, you must learn to let go of the past."

"We do not teach art here, we allow art to teach us. If you allow yourself to become so empty that the universe flows through you, your paintings will tell you stories you had never heard of. They will teach you all that you need to learn.

It is not just about creating, it is uncreating and recreating. Everything is just universal energy, and energy cannot be created or destroyed, it can only be transformed. Recreate the stories that have never been told . . . recreate the magic that you want the world to know.

Your pain and scars have led you here. The situations we go through are all a part of a grand plan to help us reach where we are destined to be.

Find a way to let go, find a way to catharsis. Let your paintings weave the magic and then the world will be a happy place again."

Out into the world

The art school had taught me a lot about the world, both the inner and the outer world. It was time for me to present all that I knew and also that which I didn't. I knew I had been prepared for this ever since I was born, perhaps even before that!

I remember the incomplete circle, a Zen symbol, that our teacher had painted and asked us to enquire unto ourselves the meaning of its incompleteness. As much as I researched, I could not fathom the true essence of what it meant. Then one day as I sat down, my mind sifted through all that I had learnt. I remembered the teacher telling us, "Write a wordless verse, paint a colourless painting, yet have the power to express the universe." How does one write a wordless verse or paint a colourless painting . . . that would be painting nothing . . .

That was it! It means silence, nothingness . . . only when we are able to paint nothingness can we paint the entire universe. Only when we understand the meaning of the spaces between words, we can harness the universal verse!

It's the void that completes the incomplete circle, because without the void everything becomes meaningless, jibber jabber, mixed shades; it's the void that gives beauty and grace to art and life!

I sit on the charpoy and cup my hands to look for the void!

It is my prayer, my gratification, my silence.

In my dreams, I have seen you . . . my dream will be true today, not because you have arrived but because I have. Now, I have finally understood and in that understanding I have become free of my past and future; of you and me!

Many nights ago under the Raatrani you gave me the courage to part with my fate and embrace my destiny . . . here I am fulfilling my promise.

If I win this . . . it will be beyond victory . . . if I lose it, it will be beyond failure . . . and yet I want to lose myself . . .

To win over . . . What an irony! This is my eternal dance that begins and ends with nothingness . . . my music that goes on, regardless the tabla beats . . . my colourless painting that has more meaning than the sacrosanct verses . . .

Tomorrow will not be the same . . . I will cease to be what I was forced to be, and become what I was destined to become. I know that you will be right beside me when I make this journey, but this is my journey . . . I need to make this alone and when I'm done, I will meet you under the Raatrani where it all started.

Kabir

I was in Paris for an Annual Writers Seminar that I had received an invite for; was it instinct or some strange law of the universe I cannot fathom, but I decided to stop by an art exhibition that featured the work of a budding Indian artist.

For a moment, I thought of Suhani; I had wanted her to find herself. I missed her every moment after she had left, yet I was happy that she was in a place she deserved to be in. Maybe someday, we would find each other again, maybe that day would be today.

I visited Benares often, even after she left. I wanted to find the Sadhu and talk to him. I somehow didn't see him again. The stories he shared with me have stayed with me all along. I write, I travel, I see . . . there are times when I hear the most profound truths and at times some lazy banter, it all seems the same these days. I know that I will meet her someday and I must wait till then. The Sadhu had told me about the spark, it is the spark that connects us and binds us and we will meet again, maybe today!

The theme was based on a few lines written just outside the gallery. Although my mind instantly recognised the artist, my heart was racing. I smiled to myself. She always spoke of serendipity; I stood there re-reading those lines, and moments seemed like aeons, going in would mean seeing her again . . .

Under the Raatrani,

I see the Moon

And an abstract effigy of dusky white lights

The threads are untangled;

The window has lost its bars

I . . . have kept my word

You're the answer to my

unanswered Prayer

I am waiting

SUHANI

F our years I had spent without him, and just when I had started to lose hope of finding him again, I saw him walk into the gallery, curiosity and anxiousness etched over his face.

I was seated at the far end of the gallery, I could easily see the visitors and see my work reflected in their eyes, but for them spotting me was close to impossible.

But not for him. He entered the gallery and his eyes found mine in one instant.

I had imagined this in my head a million times, running into him and yet remaining my calm poised self, but now when it was happening, I was losing every trace of me . . . all over again.

My palms were moist and my heart was racing; he walked towards me, his eyes not leaving mine. Those eyes told me so much. In those few seconds, we transgressed four long years; so much had changed, he looked different.

My heart and my expression must have given me away. I had dreamt of this moment a million times.

The moment had finally arrived, yet I was tied-down by unfamiliar emotions.

We were locked in a long embrace as moments passed by, nothing mattered other than him.

I let my tears fall as he said, "I kept my word too, love."

Newness and First love revisited

The next few days were a haze and yet their beautiful memories remain with me. We walked the streets of Paris, the sun gloriously shone on our happy faces. To the world we may have looked like a long married couple perhaps; only we knew we were re-discovering each other, exploring those places in each other which had changed over the years and those that we had left untouched   in the past!

We spoke about everything that had happened in the past four years and also recalled fond memories of our time in Benares.

On the first night we met, he made love to me in his hotel room that overlooked the Eiffel Tower. The little lights glittering on the streets of Paris, a light drizzle outside the window and his hands and mouth claiming every part of my body, saying so many unsaid words was magic. To have him inside of me, making me feel loved with his caresses made me feel so complete.

We lay in bed hours after we made love, saying sweet nothings to each other.

Sunshine flooding through the window woke me up, he looked older than what I had imagined, yet peaceful. It felt content to watch him asleep like shades of blue overlapping a sea of white.

Marriage

A month later, we are in New York, a place that Kabir still thinks of as his home. We are in a chapel amidst a few friends and his close family. The friends that I have made in the past have come down to celebrate this moment with me. Despite rehearsing the walk so many times, I am nervous. Never did I imagine that I would wear a white gown and walk down the aisle.

The moment has arrived, I have loved and found at last. This walk is the most difficult one yet the most memorable!

He looks at me as I walk towards him and the priest on the altar, his eyes convey that which even a thousand words cannot.

We are man and wife in that moment, bound by love for life, till the end of time, till the end of eternity.

I am married!

Waves

It's the city, thought the Sadhu . . . Benares had a divine light and energy, perhaps since the beginning of time . . . the power to send people to places on their quest . . . or bring them back . . .

He asked Meenu for another cup of chai. Meenu had taken Suhani's place at the Assi Ghat where she would sell chai and snacks to travellers . . .

He knew that he would meet them someday . . .

He was waiting . . .

SUHANI

I am in one of the world's oldest living cities, from where the dead commence their journey into the heavenly abode. However, that is not my reason of being here. I am home! The sights and smells of this city have never parted from me. Smells of burning butter in lamps; of the rock salt and cardamom in the morning tea can never leave you, if you have woken up to them for 20 years . . .

When I decided on doing a series of paintings, I knew I will conclude with the Ganges!

I am here to complete the new series of paintings that I have started, titled "Waves."

Sitting on the banks of the Nile feels different from the Ganges . . . you may say that they are geographically in different locations, but aren't they both rivers, made out of same elements, then why the difference? I believe both contain the same soul, yet their journeys are different from one another . . . maybe, that's why they seem so different on the outside. Isn't it the same with us? The journeys that we take, shape us; within, we are all light!

I tell the journalist who is sitting with me on the Assi Ghat to interview me from what she tells me will make her "Big Story."

Until about five years ago, I could have never imagined my life to be the "Big Story," the places where life takes us are strange indeed.

It is sunrise, time for those who have sinned at night to take a dip and cleanse that which they want forgotten; the Ganga miraculously accommodating millions of sins and letting them go with every passing wave. A moment of divinity; sun rays passing through dust particles making them look like thousands of souls seeking salvation just above the Ganges, somewhere faraway, a kite is seen soaring high into the clouds and seagulls fly past boatmen to the sound of what may seem like a hundred temple bells ringing to the synchronicity of an invisible orchestra. Moments of chaos are sometimes the deepest moments of peace . . .

The cameraman has adjusted his equipment, the journalist has done her final touch of make-up. I won't need any . . . colours are for my canvas is what I politely tell her when she offers me a kit.

We sit on a charpoy, while she fires rapid instructions to her crew. I carefully set out my canvas paints and brushes. This is what I have known since I was a child, my ways of understanding emotions, people, the real, unreal and the surreal. I close my eyes and see images . . . of blue black waves, tidal waves, waves of love, sorrow, defeat, hunger, pride . . . waves that wash over and refuse to grant solace . . . waves that leave you empty yet untouched . . . waves that grant wishes and redeem souls.

It's not easy to understand my view of this world. For me, nothing is black, white or grey . . . everything has infinite dimensions, layers, colours . . . everything is actively passive and yet passively active . . .

The Ganges makes me feel rooted . . . I feel like an actor who is about to deliver her part, an instrument in the hands of something far greater than the reaches and depths of my mind.

For me, everything that exists and is a part of this universe is an array of colours . . . an illusion of shades . . . a deceptive garb . . . within rests the light . . . Amma often said, everything is "Maya - Illusion."

****

About the Author

Turia is an Indian author. She is a publicist by profession. An avid reader, she loves traveling, daydreaming, and writing poetry in her free time.

Printed in the United States
By Bookmasters